Wheedle
and the Noodle

Written by **Stephen Cosgrove**
Illustrated by **Robin James**

SASQUATCH BOOKS
SEATTLE

Text copyright © 2011 by Stephen Cosgrove
Illustrations copyright © 2011 by Robin James
All rights reserved. No portion of this book may be reproduced or utilized in any form, or by any
electronic, mechanical, or other means, without the prior written permission of the publisher.

Manufactured in China by C&C Offset Printing Co. Ltd. Shenzhen, Guangdong Province, in October 2012

Published by Sasquatch Books

16 15 14 13 12   10 9 8 7 6 5 4 3 2

Cover design and interior composition: Sarah Plein
Cover and interior illustrations: Robin James
Interior design and composition: Rosebud Eustace and Rijuta Trivedi

Library of Congress Cataloging-in-Publication Data is available.

ISBN-13: 978-1-57061-730-0

Sasquatch Books
1904 Third Avenue, Suite 710
Seattle, WA 98101
(206) 467-4300
www.sasquatchbooks.com
custserv@sasquatchbooks.com

Dedicated to James, Laurie, Robby, Lauren, Evie, Jessie Rae, Dax, and Jace. They all played merrily in mind as this story did unfold.

—Stephen Cosgrove

**There's a Wheedle on the Needle
I know just what you're thinking,
But if you look up late at night
You'll see his red nose blinking.**

A nd so it was . . .

. . . and so it is to this very day that a delightful, furry creature with a big red nose called the Wheedle lived atop the Space Needle in the wonderful city of Seattle.

Each night and much of every day he slept soundly. His snarkled snores echoed softly like a storm long gone past the horizon.

Importantly, with every snore he snarkled his big red nose blinked on and off.

There were those who thought the Wheedle's real name should be Meedle. For much if not all that he did was all about *ME*—not me but him—caring about himself and very little about others.

He yelled at loggers because he hated happy whistling. He hated the sound of whistling so much that he brought rain-heavy clouds to Seattle in a giant bag. It's hard to whistle when it's raining and the Wheedle kept it raining for a long, long time. He only agreed to stop the rain when craftsmen stitched, knitted, and sewed a giant pair of earmuffs that when worn wrapped him in delightful silence.

In exchange for the earmuffs, the Wheedle kept his bargain and never made it rain for more than was needed.

In that earmuffed silence, the Wheedle slept undisturbed. Most importantly, the kindly folk of Seattle were allowed to happily whistle whenever and wherever they wished.

The story goes that the Wheedle lived at the very tippy top of the Needle.

This was and is only partially true.

For just below the very top, which of course is magically dramatic, is a hidden space called simply the attic. It was here that the Wheedle kept his favorite treasures: a toothbrush with a squiggly on the end, a lost frisbee now found, his cloud pillow, and his much-used sleeping sack.

Most importantly, the attic was where the Wheedle hid himself from the prying eyes of those who would seek to sneak an extra peek.

The biggest "me" of all was that the Wheedle loved to be alone.

All was as perfect as perfect could be and would have been that way until this very day except . . .

. . . one damp, foggy night, even through his earmuffs, the Wheedle heard a long, soft mewling sound.

"Meow! Meow!"

He woke with a "whoof" and a "wazzat?"

He listened and again, he heard it—soft as a whisper of a whistle in the wind. It wasn't a loud sound. It wasn't a bad sound. But it was a sound that woke the Wheedle. Any sound that wakes the Wheedle is not good sound, unless, of course, you really like lots of rain.

Finally, the muted mewling faded and then stopped altogether.

Satisfied that it was gone for good, the Wheedle stretched and yawned, then cozied himself back into his sleeping sack.

Just as he closed his eyes the noise again softly echoed across the city.

"Meow! Meow!"

It was a sad sound, a haunting sound, indeed. It was a "stay awake and listen to me" sound.

The Wheedle tossed. The Wheedle turned. The Wheedle tried to go back to sleep, but no matter how he tried, sleep would not come. Even with his large furry hands pressed hard against the earmuffs, the sound kept ringing in his ears.

Finally he sat up and peered up into the night.

What *was* that sound?

"Meow! Meow!"

It was apparent that no matter what, the mewling was going to continue and that sound was going to keep the Wheedle awake. Dressed in his knit stocking cap and his rainbow-colored scarf, he climbed carefully down the Needle. The Wheedle was going to find the source of the sound and stop it, once and for all.

Up and down Queen Anne Hill he searched, but nothing did he find.

He walked the shores of Lake Union and threaded his way through Belltown, and still he could not find the source of the sound. He was tired and he was grumpy as could be.

In the distance thunder rumbled.

If this kept up it would soon rain more than just a little bit in Seattle. It was going to rain a lot.

As the evening meandered past midnight and beyond, the Wheedle continued his search. He followed the sound through the maze of Pike Place Market, all the stalls and shops closed and shuttered.

He had just resolved himself to an angry sleepless night in Seattle when he saw a small, forlorn, shadowed shape sitting in the doorway of a deserted restaurant. Nailed to the door was a sign that simply read:

NONA MARIA'S CAFÉ
CLOSED FOREVER

As the fog lifted, revealing a full silvery moon, he moved closer and closer still. There, sitting beside a nearly empty bowl of noodles, was a tiny kitten. The kitten lifted its head and softly mewed.

"Meow! Meow!"

"Harumph! So it's just a little noodle of a kitten making all of this noise."

The Wheedle leaned down and put a finger to his lips.

"Shhh!" he whispered loudly. "Be quiet and go home, little Noodle. Some of us have to sleep."

The kitten, now named Noodle, softly meowed, "I would go home, but I have no home. I used to live at the café, but it's been closed forever."

"Then, silly Noodle," the Wheedle grumbled, "find yourself a *new* home. Any place will do."

With that he turned on his furry heel and went back to *his* home on the Needle.

Exhausted, the Wheedle slipped back into his sleeping sack and plopped his head onto his ever-soft cloud pillow. He had nearly fallen asleep when he felt an odd sensation on his tummy. His eyes popped open very wide. Sitting on his belly was the little kitten, Noodle.

The Wheedle propped himself up and looked down at the cat. "What are you doing here?" he said angrily. "I told you to go home."

"And I told you I didn't have one."

The Wheedle was very flustered. "And then I told you to find a new home."

"And I did."

"You mean here?" the Wheedle asked.

"It's perfect," purred the kitten. "A purrfectly perfect *new* home." And with that she bumped her head lovingly on the Wheedle's nose.

O kay! Okay! Tonight!" he muttered. "Just for tonight!" With that he scrunched back into his sack and tried to go back to sleep.

He probably would have gone to sleep, save for a furry paw that kept batting at his nose.

"Now what?" he grumbled.

"Your nose," Noodle purred, "it's blinking on and off. Now I want to play."

"No, now I want you to go to sleep."

The kitten crouched, her tail swishing back and forth. "No! I want to play." She leaped and landed with a furry thump on a big red blinking nose.

The Wheedle was buried in the muck and mire of a sticky situation.

And so they played. They played "chase the end of the Wheedle's finger." They played "pounce and bite the Wheedle's toes." They played this. They played that. They played the whole night through.

Late the next morning the Wheedle woke with the kitten purring in his arms. He gently ran his hand down Noodle's back and smiled, then yanked his hand back as if stung by a bee. He shook his head. "This isn't right! This kitty has got to go."

Woken by the rumblings, Noodle happily bumped her head against the Wheedle's cheek. "I am ever so hungry. Do you have any milk or cream?"

The Wheedle rolled his eyes and sighed a great big sigh. With the frisbee in hand he disappeared. He was back in a flash with the toy brimming with milk from the restaurant below. Noodle happily lapped at the milk while the Wheedle paced about.

"When you are finished I am taking you to the animal shelter. It's a place where orphan cats and dogs find new homes. They will find you a perfectly perfect place to live."

"But I like it here with you," mewed Noodle.

"Ah, but you will like the shelter even better."

The Wheedle scooped the kitten up into his arms and hurried down to the animal shelter, which was not far away. The kindly folk at the shelter were as nice as nice could be. They took Noodle from the Wheedle and plopped her into a cage.

Suddenly the Wheedle wasn't so sure of his decision.

"You are sure she will be adopted by a good family?" he asked nervously.

"There are no guarantees, but we are pretty sure."

A tear trickling from her eye, Noodle pressed her nose to the bars and mewed, "Bye bye, Wheedle. I love you!"

"Uh, well, I love you, too."

The Wheedle slowly backed to the door and then quickly departed, leaving Noodle to find her perfectly perfect home.

There's an old saying that once bumped on the nose by a kitten, you can never get it out of your heart. In the face of this old saying, the Wheedle went back to the Needle, pulled on his well-worn earmuffs and flopped down on his sleeping sack. Eager to regain the sleep he had lost, he closed his eyes and waited for the dreams to come.

And waited.

And waited.

And waited.

He finally got up and climbed to the very top of the Needle. There he sat wrapped in his seclusion as the sun began to set, a lonely sight, indeed.

Still and all, in time a little kitten called Noodle did find the most perfect of perfectly perfect places to stay. And with her new family she lived happily ever after.

Wheedle and the Noodle
Happy in their home,
They live upon on the Needle
Neither to be alone.

About the Author

I have spent my life as a dream-maker. To be able to crawl inside a story as it is being created is an unbelievable and delightful experience. By reading this book and others that I have written, you are able to share my experiences. I have written and published 320 books or so, and it is only by the grace of God that I continue this amazing adventure.

—Stephen Cosgrove

About the Illustrator

I have been drawing since I could hold a pencil.

After illustrating more than 80 books over the past 35 years, I realize there is no greater joy than doing what I love and knowing it may bring a smile to someone's face. It's the icing on the cake of life.

—Robin James